COPPELIA

Illustrated by
KRYSTYNA TURSKA

Text by Linda M. Jennings

SILVER BURDETT COMPANY

MORRISTOWN, NEW JERSEY

Library of Congress Cataloging-in-Publication Data
Jennings, Linda M.
     Coppelia.

     Summary: A dollmaker cleverly schemes to pass
his most beautiful doll off as a real girl, but he
is outwitted by the townspeople he tries to deceive.
     [1. Fairy tales. 2. Dolls–Fiction. 3. Ballets–Stories,
plots, etc.] I. Turska, Krystyna,
1933–   ill.   II. Title.
PZ8.J372Co 1985   [E]   86–3748
ISBN 0-382-09241-4

Text copyright © 1985 Hodder and Stoughton Ltd
Illustrations copyright © 1985 Krystyna Turksa

First published 1985

Text by Linda M. Jennings

Published in the United States
in 1986 by Silver Burdett Company,
Morristown, New Jersey

Printed in Belgium by Henri Proost & Cie,
Turnhout

Once upon a time there lived a strange and
sinister-looking old man called Dr. Coppelius.

Some laughed at him, and some were even
frightened of his peculiar appearance.
No one knew exactly what he did, or what he
worked at late into the night when a light
could be seen gleaming from an upper window
of his house.

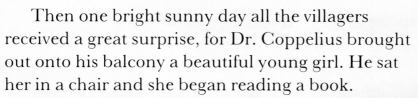

Then one bright sunny day all the villagers received a great surprise, for Dr. Coppelius brought out onto his balcony a beautiful young girl. He sat her in a chair and she began reading a book.

Not an expression flickered on her pretty peaches-and-cream face as young Swanilda shouted up to her:

"Come down to meet my friends."

But the beautiful young girl never stirred.

Next on the scene was Franz, Swanilda's fiancé, and it was plain he was more than taken with the occupant of the balcony. He lingered underneath, gazing up at her and smiling, until old Dr. Coppelius shouted at him to go away. Still the young girl sat reading, unperturbed by the angry words.

Swanilda was furious with her fiancé for his attentions to the young girl, whom they had named "Coppelia" after the old doctor.

"It's nothing, I was curious, that's all," said Franz.
Swanilda refused to listen, and burst into tears
when the Mayor announced that he would give a
bag of gold to every couple married on the day
a new bell was to be presented to the
village church.

"Small chance there will be of receiving *that*,"
she cried, running away from Franz, who still stood,
pleading with her.

"Come back, don't let's quarrel," he cried.

But Swanilda was gone.

Despite the quarrel Franz was determined to enjoy himself. That evening there were festivities in the Square, and the young couples danced, drank and sang until dusk — without Swanilda.

Franz joined in the merry dances, and it seemed as though he had completely forgotten his unhappy fiancée.

As darkness fell a door opened in Dr. Coppelius's house,
and the old man emerged, shuffling down the street.
He carried an enormous key with him, and he had
not gone far before he was spotted by a group of
high-spirited youths, Franz among them.

They immediately flocked around him, jeering and
jostling.

"Be off with you," cried Dr. Coppelius,
waving his stick at them.

Laughing loudly, the youths danced back into the
Square again.

Along the selfsame street Swanilda now came with
some of her girlfriends.

Suddenly she stumbled over an object in the road.

"What is it?" asked the girls curiously.

"Why, an old key," replied Swanilda.

They had come to a halt outside Dr. Coppelius's house.
"What if it fits the Doctor's door?" she joked.
"Shall we try it?"

As Swanilda so rightly guessed the key did fit
Dr. Coppelius's heavy door. It creaked open and
the girls crept stealthily inside, peering into the gloom.
Giggling, they all climbed the stairs, and then
came to a stop.

For in the room at the top were a number of small,
mysterious-looking figures.

"Why, they are mechanical toys," said Swanilda.
"Let's wind them up."

As her friends set all the clockwork toys in motion
Swanilda opened the doors to the balcony where earlier
the strange and beautiful Coppelia had sat reading.
The girl was still there, sitting in the chair with
her book.

Swanilda suddenly shook her by the shoulders.
Coppelia rocked to and fro, and then toppled over.
    "Why she's only a doll, too," cried Swanilda, laughing.
"Oh now I can think of a grand joke to play!"

Meanwhile, outside the house, Dr. Coppelius was
frantically searching for his key.
So intent was he on his task that he failed to notice
Franz, who had propped a ladder against the house,
and was now starting to climb up it.

By the time Franz had reached the room upstairs, all the
clockwork toys had run down, and the girls had fled.

But alas for Franz, the old doctor had succeeded in
getting into his house, and now stood in the middle of the
room.

He opened his mouth to shout at the frightened youth,
but a better plan suddenly came to him.
Suppose, just suppose, he could steal Franz's
life force and transfer it to his precious doll,
Coppelia. Why then he would have a real live
daughter of his own! He smiled and offered Franz
a chair and a glass of drugged wine.

Excited by this plan, Coppelius rushed to the balcony and brought in his beautiful doll.
As Franz sat dazed by the wine and by the sight of the lovely Coppelia, the old Doctor sat at the table, muttering the spell that would transform the doll into a living girl.

It seemed he had succeeded, too, for Coppelia
started to move and pose a foot, as if to dance.
Now she was well and truly alive.
She danced and twirled round the room,
she performed Spanish flamencos and Scottish flings.
Her movements became wilder and wilder, as she
waltzed up to Franz and shook him from his dull stupor.
And then from the balcony came an anguished cry.

Dr. Coppelius had discovered his doll, lying lifeless and naked on the chair.

The dancing Coppelia was none other than Swanilda, who had dressed herself in Coppelia's clothes to trick him!

Swanilda's clever trick had reconciled the
young couple, and several days later they were married.

And now they stood in the village Square, hand-in-
hand, to receive the bag of gold from the Mayor.
"The bag of gold must go to Dr. Coppelius," said Franz,
"for we treated him very badly."

But the Mayor was determined that all should be
happy on this joyous day.

Dr. Coppelius received his bag of gold,
but so did Franz and Swanilda.

And the new church bell rang out in the clear
morning air to celebrate the wedding.